# THE BOY I MET ON THE ISLAND

STAR GIRL

Made with ♥ on the Notion Press Platform
www.notionpress.com

This book is dedicated to ones who believe
in love, who long for stability and
happiness in their life and to the ones
searching for a change that could lead to
something beautiful

# Contents

# Legal Copyright

# Preface

**For the readers :**
Born in Delhi (India) with a nuclear family, I've thought I could have a simple life, I really love to read novels, books since childhood, it inspires me in every way. Years later, when I've started reading interactive stories, they gave me a whole new direction and made me decide to be an author and writing became fun and enjoyable just like a friend you always need. In 2019 starting with my first interactive story "A cold bad heart" from Episode app and then later A rooftop neighbor from Wattpad app and some other stories like My mystery man, Accidentally star, Rock star near me, Mr. hunk and more from the Dorian : comics you play app. Apart from this Korean drama, Manga are my inspiration.

"**The Boy I Met On The Island**" is a short novel about independency, freedom and love with simple, calm and peaceful vibes. A successful woman searching for her love which she left behind years ago.

I hope the story would be fun and entertaining with a touch of drama, action and a bit of romance for all the readers reading this.

# Acknowledgements

*There are some people names whom I really want to include and want to acknowledge for their faith and love in me and also their putting hard work and dedication in contents of this book.*

*My Sister Miss Ankita who really love, support and also motivated me to write. She is always been my idol.*

*My best friend Dr. Sadhna who supported and motivated me throughout in making and being my inspiration.*

*And at last My brother who supported me and motivate to write and follow my dreams.*

*Also, I like to give my thanks to my parents who have been an inspiration for me working hard, raising me and supported me wherever possible.*

*I am very thankful to some of my other friends whether they are from my school, college even my workplaces or outside India*

*A special thanks to my another best friend Miss Daniela from Denmark (Germany) even if we were far away she still supported me in every way starting from episode app to this novel and so on.*

# CHAPTER ONE

# An Opportunity Of Luck

Me and Jacob were sitting on a sea shore, the weather was bright and beautiful just like a bright camera filter. The water makes waves and ripples washing away the stones.

We were teenage kids who were the only ones on the island, those times we always stood for each other in the worst times.

I remember everything like old times. I was looking out the window when my chauffeur looked at me for a moment and said, "Miss, what were you thinking so deeply?"

It has been five years now, but I still remember him clearly. He is handsome, and glowing, with tousled hair and small hands. He is a little bit grumpy, too, and he also wears a star-shaped necklace.

He was so alluring with bright blue eyes that I couldn't take my eyes off him

If anyone asks whats my story then I'll say **my story - its romantic with different worlds,** we dont belong to each other and yet we want to be.

I have everything like literally everything - **Money, Fame, and Love** andrecently dating a millionaire for 3 years but I don't feel so happy talking to him, he has always been very busy and never got time for me.

Honestly, I wanted to leave everything behind because nothing matters to me anymore.

**If I could go back to the island again, would I be happy?**

A few weeks later, I got the opportunity to research the same island for the establishment of my new hotel. I was very happy when my father discussed it, he said I could study there for 3-6 months which gave me a chance to see him again.

I went to share the news with my fiance about the hotel but when I reached the door, I heard him talking to his PS (Personal Secretary) *"Our company **COUTURE** has been in a big crisis, we need urgent 238k dollars to invest"* she said

*"Don't worry, I'll sell some of her shares,"* he said thinking

The secretary was surprised to hear *"But..your fiancee, isn't that too much that you are holding her company shares?"*

He laughed walking with his hands behind *"She is my fiancee, of course she can allow **A little help** to me"*

I looked at him angrily hiding *"How could he use my money like that?"* I mumbled

I walked towards him and broke up straight without listening to his excuses, and then I went out from his office *"I need to relax"* I said sighing.

I again remembered about a project for my hotel I had planned immediately to leave for the unknown island where I spent my time 5 years ago.

I called my pilot to get the helicopter ready and with that, I left it in the helicopter for the island to see him

It was still noon, the sun shone brightly, and the sky and water were blue as I looked around

*"It's been 3 months since you called me miss, is everything fine?"* he said

*"Yeah, everything is fine it's just I need a break for a moment,"* I said concerning his question *"Can you drop me there?"* I added

*"But miss, how will you survive without a network here?"* he said with a surprised expression

*"I'll be fine, my father will handle everything,"* I said jumping carefully handling some suitcase with me as he dropped me there helping with the bags

I looked at the sea, it's beautiful like an aquamarine with calm tides moving. Immediately I cover my head with a hat going towards the jungle area to look for him but it's getting harder

I keep on exploring seeing the amazing scenery of the jungle, some tribal men and women around here.

I went close to them asking about the little boy showing them a photo on my phone.

They were surprised and deny it about him which makes me feel losing my hope, a purpose to see whom I left behind

*"How is he? how does he look now? will he still remember me?"* I keep mumbling about it without thing going towards a deep forest

There was a cave and I went inside with my lost mind and saw golden amber eyes in dark

As far as I remember, his eyes were light blue then who is he

I came close to my eyes to see and see the figure of a lion, my body went white instantly as he roared and I immediately ran out from the cave towards the forest.

I kept running from him but his speed was very fast compared to mine then I saw the arrow towards me but it passed from me piercing the lion's chest

I looked around and saw Jacob closely with a bow in his hand, bare-chested, with a bit long hair, and as usual, his body was still glowing and his eyes were as blue as the sea here.

"*We finally meet Jacob,*" I said in my mind silently.

# CHAPTER TWO

# Jacob

Our eyes were inseparable from looking at each other. The man I wanted to see is in front of me. He reminds me of 5 years ago when we were teenage kids.

We used to build sand castles together, go to the beach together running, laughing. It was fun being around him.

Those time I was been lost through the dense jungle for 2 months when my parents and I went to holiday, it was summer vacation in may and june and then my parents had to call rescue team when they found me fell down from a trap in the forest.

Its a very long story for another time but right now all I see is him and definately he is changed as he is not the same boy with whom I roam around.

He is still glowing, his hairs were in a black mess but they can get perfectly straight, his eyes are shining bright like the sea blue with a little green shade. I can see his star shaped necklace on his neck down to his broad chest as he crosses his arms looking at me

*"What are you looking at?"* he said being rude to me

I didn't expect him to be this rude *"Don't you remember me Jacob?"* I said patting my chest voluntary to make him recognize him

He looked at me for a moment and said *"No, if you are interested in me then I'll refuse"* he said

I sigh as it looks like he completely forgotten about me but thats not his fault here, we may have to start things again then I cleared my throat, *"I am dahlia, owner of a multinational company. I came to see the space for my project, dont worry everyone here is gonna get the benefit, i promise"* i said

He got startled with my name for a moment then get back to his normal self *"I refuse for this project"* he said

*"Hey, it wont be bad.. you may can lot of advantages for that"* i said trying to persude him

*"No"* he said

*"But why? don't you want more people to come here?"* i said thinking

*"I still refuse because its our birthplace and we can't allow any changes to do here"* he said

I sigh maybe I should take things slow *"So, where do you live now?"* i said changing the topic

*"At my home"* he said then few minutes later an old came beating him

*"You rascal, answer her properly"* she said in her shaking voice

*"Nana, why are you here?"* he said

*"Nana?"* i said

The old lady smiles *"Im his grandmother not by blood but he saved me from beasts from that day I became his Nana"*

*"Oh, nice to meet you Nana"* I said bowing down

*"What a beautiful girl doing here?"* she said in cracked voice

*"I came to see space for my project"* i said

*"Ah, the space..I am very sorry my dear we cant give you any space here to start your project. The reason is this land is*

*of Jacob's father, he was also a big enterpreneur like you but for this land, his enemies killed Jacob's parents. It is said there is a treasure inside the water"* she said

*"Nana, you don't need to tell everything to her"* he said angrily

I feel startled with the old lady said *"Treasure?"* I kept mumbling

*"Yes, treasure my dear but nobody knows where it is exactly"* she said

*"Nana, thats enough"* he said angrily

*"And you? I think you should go back as we can't give you the land here"* he said

I was about to leave but then Nana stops me *"young girl, you must be tired, you can rest at our place"* she said

*"Nana, this is too much giving shelter to a stranger"* he said

*"Shut up you Rascal"* she said beating him with the stick

*"Guess I have no choice "* I said turning towards the jungle area walking with them

We kept walking as I looked at Jacob who is in dilemma, lost in thinking to himself

# CHAPTER THREE

# Nana's Home

Jacob kept being silent till we reached his home

The home is made of glass which is quite durable and cannot be easily broken.

Nana welcomed me opening the gate and we got entered inside

The interior of this home was very unique, it was made up of colorful shells, cream paint and white on the gates and windows. It wasn't the ordinary home like I've seen but it was the most comfortable place.

I sat on the wooden chair as they offer me some fruits for appetizer which I enjoyed a lot

He looked at me for a moment then he felt silent again.

Nana looked at him and said *"So dear, Is the project the only thing which made you came here?"*

I almost choke drinking water and coughed where as Jacob looked at me awkwardly

He stands coming closer looking at me *"Are you okay? Is there anything?"*

I drank water slowly then said *"No, everything is fine. Nana, I just came for the project, once it is finished then I'm going to leave from here"*

He frowns for a moment then leave to his room

Nana looked at him *"Sorry my dear you have to see this, he is always like this ever since his parents abandoned him"*

*"Abandoned? I remember his father was a big businessman"* I said surprisingly

She remembers something and said *"You must be that girl who went missing for a long time, no wonder you looked familiar and now you have grown in such a fine woman"*

She again continued explaining me *"My dear, when you left this island, his father slowly taking debts and starting gambling, going in casinos. His luck has never been good so, he couldn't pay the debts and getting so much poor that he couldn't even afford his own medicines"*

*"But then he left jacob because he couldn't pay his debts then I took Jacob with me as I worked hard slowly clearing up his debts then settling in this island since then"* she added

*"I had no idea that he faced a lot since I left"* I said startled

*"I have a question for you my dear"* she said

Few minutes later, I went to the room which she gave me and sat on the bed thinking about what nana said

*"If you came for only project then its fine but if you came for Jacob then you should tell him"* she said

But now thinking about this, I actually came to see him but things doesn't turn out that way, does he still remembers me?

I changed my dress laying down on bed as the tiredness getting close and all i could do is sleep

I woke up in mid having habit of working at night, stretching my legs then opened the door looking around for water

I went to kitchen to see Jacob half naked with only shorts drinking water from refridgerator, he eyed on me for a moment then after drinking he gave the bottle to me *"Thirsty?"* he said in low voice

I nodded taking water from him then drinking
*"How come you are not sleeping?"* I said
He looked at me and said *"There was an annoying girl who kept me awake today"* he said smirking
*"Well whom are you calling annoying?"* I said displeased
*"I can't tell beautiful"* he said walking away
I looked confused as if he fooled me or appreciated me
That was the first time he responded to me

# CHAPTER FOUR

# Island Beauty

After that night, we opened up a little bit and next day me, Nana and Jacob went to the land which is suitable for construction.

It was truely breathtaking, it was sunny with cool winds blowing faster and I hold my hat not to get swept away with the wind.

I took some snaps of the land sending to father for approval with 1 bar signal then we went for the beach.

Nana laid down on the beach relaxing on the chair while Jacob went for swim and my eyes were on the phone looking for his reply.

Few minutes later, my father replied *"Are you sure about this?"* he texted

*"Yes dad, I'm confident about it, this must be the place"* I replied

*"If thats my daughter wants"* He replied after my text

I was smiling looking at the phone then I saw Jacob coming out from the water, his wet body glowing with water droplets

He came close to me *"What makes you smile a lot?"* he said trying to see her phone

*"What the- Jacob stop!"* I said surprised as he gave a mini heart attack

*"I just want to see what you're hiding?"* he said taking my phone from me smoothly

*"Hey, give it back"* I almost yelled at him but he went towards the water

*"Not until you tell me"* he said

*"Are you nuts? you're going to drop my phone in the water?"* I panicked walking towards him

*"I said give it back!"* I said with anger surrounded me

He looked at me coldly taking glance of my text from my father, he frowned realising what he did wrong

Then he gave her phone at last saying *"I'm sorry, I was wrong getting jealous for no reason"* he said bowing down and left in the jungle

Nana woke up *"Is there something wrong between you two?"* She asked

*"Nana, it's nothing"* I said leaving towards Nana's house

That night we didn't talk and I focused on the project faster, working on the architecture designs of the hotel, problems to make salty water suitable for drinking, planning for making tourism better.

Next day, we started with the construction with the workers which were sent by my father. I explained my planning and expectations we have.

Jacob was silently looking at the construction without looking at me.

It took **8** hours with the structure and some unfinished work which they do tomorrow.

Time passes faster and its been 2 months working on the construction of hotel. The whole structure was ready only needed to plaster and paint.

That night we had dinner Nana looked at me and asked *"You're going to leave once the project is completed, as far as I know my dear in 1 month your work will be completed, am I right?"*

I nodded without looking at jacob who stepped out from the dining table to his room

I followed him in silence.

When I reaached his door, he was already standing there waiting.

He didn't smile, he didn't speak right away, the silence between us stretched and then he said it, barely above whisper: *"Dahlia"*

I looked up startled

***"If i asked you to stay... would you stay?"*** He said

My breath caught hearing his words but before I could say a word, he turned and close the door behind him.

# CHAPTER FIVE

# New Hotel

Next day in the morning I was eating my breakfast of bacon and egg thinking about Jacob thinking about the night when Jacob asked me if I could stay.

For me it was surprising, few with each other which keeps me thinking about the dumbest fight we had.

In the end the day finally came for the inauguration of new hotel the various guest for invite for this moment

Everyone except my father who had to go for very urgent work, so instead of him I will cut the ribbon symbolising for the establishment of the new hotel.

Jacob was taking care of the guest and Nana who wants to relax laid down in one of the room.

There in the evening the inauguration was put to end. Nana who was already asleep there and I talk to the employees to take care of her while me and Jacob has to go back to the house it was night when we reach to our house to take bath and change of clothes.

As I got ready comma I went to the dinner table and saw Jacob in the front of in front of me sitting, we ate dinner silently and awkwardly without talking.

The cloud were getting darker and darker as the storm was approaching and after the age the lights went out.

I can see the weather through the window as I went toward it touching the glass looking Jacob followed me curiously looking what I am seeing suddenly they is a thunder of lights strikening with **boom** sound I got scared holding Jacob.

Jacob hug me lovingly whispering*"it's just thunder"* it was the same old time when I get scared of thunder, he holds me and comforts me.

The weather was so fine that we look at each other for the moment then he released from his arms looking at me.

I didn't knew that time our lips where few inches apart but then lightning strike from the window making us aware.

It was awkward moment that we shared in that night Jacob looked at me and speak ***"your project is close to end, will you go out or stay with me?"***

I frown with the big project came to an end but still I want to stay with him I tried to speak but it ends with the silence.

I leave him going to my room with unspoken answers and a long silence.

# CHAPTER SIX

# Leaving You

According to the time I given to my father with promise was over. It's been complete three months and I am ready to leave I look that Jacob who didn't says anything then he called me in his room.

He stands on the wall looking at me *"Have you decided to go from here?"*

I looked at him as my expression falters *"Its true"* I said

He sighs and came closer to me whispering ***"If you want to leave then go but if you can't then I won't let you go"*** then he added ***"What if I loved you all along?"*** he says kissing on my cheeks

I was startled regretting with my decision but it was already decided as I told him

He kept distance from us *"Thats all I want to say"* he said giving me my luggage

I went downstairs taking my luggage ready to face the reality which I left behind and I need to look for my business too.

Another driver on the helicopter came to me to pick me up from the island, I glanced Nana and him, she smiles at me involuntary reassuring that she will talk to him.

I went inside the helicopter stealing a glance of his reaction, it was cold and uncaring.

Then the helicopter went up and the wind below it blows faster forming a circular motion.

After a week later, I got adapted with my own regular life

Paparazzi swarms around me again talking about the establishment of new hotel, that time my ex came again stealing the spotlight holding me but I pushed him away leaving him with bunch of them.

I came back to my room relaxing then my father called me congratulating for the new hotel but my mind wanders as if I am not happy like it's been sucked out from me.

That time in my mind all I can think of jacob of how we met, how he saw me for first time, how he reacts to the things. The outcome doesn't came out as I expected.

I was still thinking about whether I should stay here comfortably or go back to the Island for him leaving everything behind

To be honest, for me it was a tough decision but still my mind is filled all about him

That night it was hard for me to sleep, I kept tossing and turning thinking about Nana and him and how we were together as a family.

I remember him hugging me when lightening strikes and how he still knows that I am scared of lightening.

We were so close but still we feel some sense of miscommunication which we didn't wanted

*"I can't accept this kind of comfortable life anymore"* I said to myself sighing

But then a thought strikes in my mind **if I'll go there again, will he accept me?**

I realised that I was such a fool that I went to the island not for the project but for him all along

Next day I woke up in the morning packing my bags again to leave but then my father came to see me *"Is there's something wrong dear?"*

*"Dad, I'm going back to the Island again"* I said making decision

He looked startled and asked me for what reason I am leaving?

I told him everything and said *"For him"*

He was silent but can see the love and despiration in my eyes, he smiled at me and said "It must be about Jacob right?"

It was surprising for me but still I was happy saying thank you to him.

# CHAPTER SEVEN

# Back To You

Few hours later, coming back to island I went straight to Nana's house but it was empty.

I keep looking around to see anyone but instead I felt pair of arms around me whispering to my ears *"Shh..it's me"* he said in a very calm voice

I turn around to see who was there and I saw Jacob who was shirtless

*"W..What are you doing?"* I got startled and said awkwardly

He looked at me and said *"That is supposed to be my line, what are you doing here?"*

*"Jacob.."* I paused after realizing that he is the reason I came back

Then I immidietly hugged him and surprisingly, he held me back not letting me go

*"You know I missed you and Nana as well"* I said

He looked at me holding my hand *"I thought you will never come back"* he said

***"Why wouldn't I came after listening to my heart?"***I said

***"you know, I never left you ever since we were kids and I still say that I've loved you all along"*** he said

I felt awkward with his confession and trying to turn my head away then I realised to change the topic

*"Where's Nana? I didn't saw her ever since I came here"* I said

He turned serious but remained calm *"About her, let me tell you something"* he said gesturning to get inside

I entered in his house and saw Nana working with some papers, it were scattered around in her dining table

He came close then spoke *"Me and Nana still working to establish our old business which we lost after dad"*

*"That's amazing, I can help you in some cases if you want"* I said excitedly

He smiles nodding in approval

That night we were working together but then Nana feels tired going to her room resting leaving me and him

After few more hours, it was middle of the night, he looked at me and said *"Why did you left there and came all the way here?"*

I took a deep breath as he kept asking me again and again and then I answered him *"I came because of you Jacob, only for you"*

After that I took a pause then again continued **"when I came back, I felt everything empty and dry without you"**

I blush hesitating but he came close to me *"then why didn't you came here sooner when I asked you?"* he said

**"Because I needed to figure out my feelings for you, I needed to see if you still think about me, care for me just like old times?"** I said

**"Well of course i'll do it in a heartbeat, why couldn't I? you're always in my heart and in my mind"** he said getting closer

I blush again for the moment and came closer to him

Then he give a peck on my lips then took a step back

**"You know this is not going to be enough for me"**he said then stands up from the chair where we were working then walking towards me taking in his arms

This time I didn't hesitate or push him away, all I did is kept looking at him.

He was still shirtless with a comfy pants taking me to his room

I could stare in his blue eyes which were shinning in the moonlight, our face were close kissing, holding and immersed with love and emotions.

I have no idea how many times we panted, gasped or made sounds but all I could think is about him.

Next day in the morning I woke up with a call, it was of my ex-fiance who wants me to get married

I looked him beside me sleeping peacefully but I can tell now that I am in a big messy situation right now.

# CHAPTER EIGHT

# The Choice My Heart Fixed On

I feel stressed early in the morning due to a jerk with whom I didn't broke up properly, after calling he kept texting me if I'm okay, if i'm sleeping or eating all at once.

He also texted me that we are getting married tomorrow and with that I kept my phone aside as it is consuming my thoughts

Then my gaze was on Jacob who was sleeping peacefully, I came closer to him but then his eyes open pulling me down and close to him

*"Why were you looking so intensely at my face?"* he said smirking

I blush as I got caught, *"Its nothing"* I said turning my face away from him

He gets on top of me grabbing my face close to him smiling

*"Really? its nothing for you after what we did yesterday?"* he said laughing

I felt awkward and said *"dont talk about that"*

His attention got caught when he sees her phone with miss call of a man, he got serious and said *"who is he?"*

I sigh getting caught and said *"well, he is just a very disturbing person my ex-fiance with whom I didn't broke up properly"* trying to explain about him

*"How can he be your ex-fiance when you didn't broke up with him?"* he said looking at me seriously

I slapped my forehead in disappointment saying *"I'll break up with him properly this time"*

He crossed his arms in disappointment, *"So, you're gonna leave me again?"*

I looked at him pulling his face close to me ***"listen, we have faced a lot together and this time we will be together, I'm not going to leave you again, could you trust me this time?"*** I said looking straight to his shining blue eyes

He sighs and nodded *"Fine, break up with him this time but before you do, let me know your plans first"* he said getting out of his bed

*"Good thing is today I have a press conference about tomorrow's marriage"* I said smiling and holding his hand

Few minutes later, I came out of bed with him then I looked at him

We kiss for a moment then I said *"I'll be leaving today but I'll be back again after settling down everything"* I said

He nodded understanding me and then helping me in packing bags

Few hours later, I went in the helicopter dressed up in a white dress with orange patterns till my calf length. The ride was silent but not beats of my heart to end things fast

After few more hours, I came directly to join the press conference and all the reporters were swarming and snapping photos.

My ex-fiance was very happy to see me and showing the reporters that we are still in love.

I feel uncomfortable around him then the press conference has started with bombardment of questions

*"How do you feel marrying a billionaire miss Dahlia?"* first reporter asked

*"How is your wedding preparations going miss?"* another one asked

*"Where did you plan to go honeymoon miss Dahlia?"* and another reporter asked

My ex-fiance smiles and whispers *"Answer them"*

I smile answering *"Sorry, this wedding is cancelled"*

The reporters, paparazzi and my ex-fiance were stunned, as I ran the reporters and paparazzi ran towards me but my ex grabbed me and said *"why?"*

I was in a hurry so I told him that I love someone else releasing his hand with resistance running towards the back door

I came out of the place and saw my father, he laughed seeing me what I did

*"I've seen lot of people being crazy in love but today I witnessed it"* he said standing close to his car with with his arms crossing

*"Dad..."* I said

*"Did you finally decided to leave this place for him? I must say my daughter is getting bolder, so when am I gonna meet him?"* he said smirking

*"Dad, I'll be leaving today"* I said

*"I'm coming with you"* he said

I nodded getting inside his car

Few hours later, it was evening and we were in helicopter, the ride was silent and I looked at the places below the sky. It was beautiful with some colored lights

Few hours later, we reached to the place and saw Nana and Jacob looking at us

She looked at my father closely remembering old times
*"You're Robin right?"* she said

# CHAPTER NINE

# Familiar Faces

He looked at Nana and said, *"Yes, I'm Robin... but how do you know?"*

She said *"My son Alex always talks about you."*

He was surprised hearing Alex's name. *"You're Alex's mother?"* he asked, startled.

Nana nodded. *"Yes, I'm his mother."*

Jacob and I were looking at each other, as we have no idea as we were completely clueless.

Robin then suggested we go to the beach, and I nodded, leaving their little reunion behind.

We went to the beach as usual, he went shirtless, just in his swimming trunks.

I walked to the beach in my dress, slipping off my heels and holding them taking it aside

He came closer, splashing water, and we kept playing with laughter and soaked clothes.

Time passes by and the night came, We were having dinner. Nana and Robin were deep in conversation.

*"Do you remember my son?"* Nana asked. *"You always go swimming there with him when you two were 25, new in business,"* she added.

*"Yeah,"* he said, *"I still remember those old times. We enjoyed a lot."*

They kept chatting like a long-lost mother and son finally reunited.

Jacob and I looked at each other, awkwardly as if we didn't want to get involved.

Then Jacob looked at me while eating and asked, *"So... did you break up with him?"*

*"Yeah,"* I smiled. *"I couldn't wait to see you anymore... so I ended things quickly."*

He smiled while eating, as if he finally felt peace.

Next day in the morning, news flashed about me visiting the island with Jacob, photos of us at the beach were everywhere.

Reporters were in chaos: *"Miss Dahlia's secret admirer? Did she leave her ex-fiancé for him?"*

I woke up late, checking my phone. The news had spread like wildfire.

My friends who only cares about my money wouldn't stop calling *"Who is this man with you? He's so hot!"*

The whole phone is filled with comments on social media as I sighed. *"Just gimme a break."*

Even my ex-fiancé called to ask if it was true saying *"Did you forget already that we were supposed to get married?"* he asked.

*"Did you forgot that I'm done with you,"* I said loudly.

*"But did you leave me because of him? Who is he? Do you think he's better than me?"* he kept insisting

*"That's none of your concern,"* I snapped, hanging up the call.

Just then, my dad walked in my room to talk and I said sighing *"I know, Dad,"* I sighed. *"It's all over the social media."* I added

*"The reporters will be coming here in a few minutes,"* He said looking at me

Nana and Jacob came to my room looking at each other, then at me. *"Don't worry, we'll figure something out,"* Nana said calmly.

Jacob came close to me and whispered,*"What if we tell them we're getting married?"*

*"What?! But... isn't it too soon?"* I asked him with blushing

He knelt down in front of me and said,*"Marry me, Dahlia. I promise I'll take good care of you."*

It was a shocking moment kneeling and proposing right in front of my father but then I smiled saying yes to him.

Then few minutes later the reporters swarmed at my house.*"Miss Dahlia, can you tell us about your lover's identity?"* they asked.

I was not afraid in front of their questions so I smiled, holding his hand. *"He is my fiancé Jacob and soon to be my husband,"* I said answering them

The reporters were stunned as they got a new fresh opportunity but then one of them asked *"What about your ex-fiancé?"*

I smile answering them poudly still holding his hand *"It's none of my concern anymore. Everyone is invited to my wedding tomorrow,"*

# CHAPTER TEN

# Wedding

The invitations were distributed to the media, paparazzi, and all our family and friends.

Jacob and I were holding hands when Nana barged in, *"It's your wedding day, and you two are still sitting like this?"*

Then looking at us she laughed. *"My lovely dears, it's time for you both to get dressed up!"*

She pulled us apart, saying, *"I'm taking Dahlia with me, so you go get ready."*

Jacob smiled looking at me then sighed, *"Fine, grandma."*

Meanwhile, my father and his friends were admiring the decoration work.

One of Jacob's friends looked at him and said, *"Robin, the decoration looks great! But where's the priest?"*

*"He's coming in five minutes, he is on the way,"* he replied to his friend

Few minutes later, after the decorations were completed, his friend glanced with twinkle in his eyes, the beach venue was magical with sea shells, corals, and pastel-colored decorations everywhere. including soft shades of purple, pink, and sky blue made it feel like a dream.

Jacob stood at the altar in an expensive suit, looking handsome as ever waiting

A few minutes later, the priest arrived. *"Sorry for the delay,"* he said.

*"Where's the bride?"* then he asked the groom.

Moments later, my father walked in holding my hand walking Down the Aisle

I wore a small white gown with coral-pink roses delicately sewn into the fabric.

Jacob looked at me, surprised and completely taken.

Once I stand in the alter, he walked closer, leaned in and whispered, **"You look beautiful."**

I blushed hearing his voice, it was low and husky, the kind that could make any woman weak in the knees.

I tried to keep my cool, pretending to fix my dress and looking down, but he chuckled softly, making it worse then he whispered again, **"You know that's really cute,"** and with that I nearly melted from embarrassment.

The priest asked us to say our vows. We placed the rings on each other's fingers with shaking hands and full hearts.

Reporters were busy capturing the moment flashes, cameras, murmurs but it was just us, in our little bubble.

We smiled, exchanging our vows.

*"You may kiss the bride,"* the priest finally said.

Jacob looked at me, leaned in, and kissed me gently. It felt like the world paused. Everyone cheered for us

It was the best decision I ever made, marrying my childhood friend who stood up for me, **the boy I met on the island.**

Our married life was peaceful. Nana spent more time with us, and my father helped with our business while giving us space in our own home. We were inseparable including our hands on each other

A few years later, the number one reporter asked us for a press conference.

We stood there, holding hands in public, smiling as we talked about our love story.

Everyday was joyful event for us but not for for everyone

My ex was drowning in tears after realizing how guilty he felt for using me, but it was too late. His secretary had already stayed with him too long.

People say the story ends here, But I say...

**This is just the beginning of a new life.**

*THE END*

# Author's Note

*Thank you so much for reading **The Boy I Met On The Island.** This story mainly written for everyone including the young adults who wants love and stability in their lives. This is my first time writing a novel like this which includes slice of life.*

*It means a lot to me if you can leave reviews on my instagram handle*

*Also Can Follow Me On Instagram :* **sg.stories_94**

*More stories like Stranger things between us, A rooftop neighbour in novel coming soon. Please stay tuned for more*